Good
Night

This book belongs to

Good
Night

GOOD NIGHT,

This is the original 1985 hardcover book,
completely redrawn by the author for its 36th Anniversary.

Little Simon
An imprint of Simon & Schuster Children's Publishing Division
New York London Toronto Sydney New Delhi • 1230 Avenue of the Americas, NY, NY 10020
Copyright © 1982, 1985, 1995, 2019, 2021 by Sandra Boynton. All rights reserved, including the right of reproduction
in whole or in part in any form. LITTLE SIMON is a registered trademark of Simon & Schuster, Inc.,
and associated colophon is a trademark of Simon & Schuster, Inc.
ISBN 978-1-5344-9974-4   Printed in China 0721 SCP
10 9 8 7 6 5 4 3 2

GOOD NIGHT

BASED ON *The Going to Bed Book*

by Sandra Boynton

For Caitlin, Keith, Devin, and Darcy
who are never tired

The sun has set
not long ago.

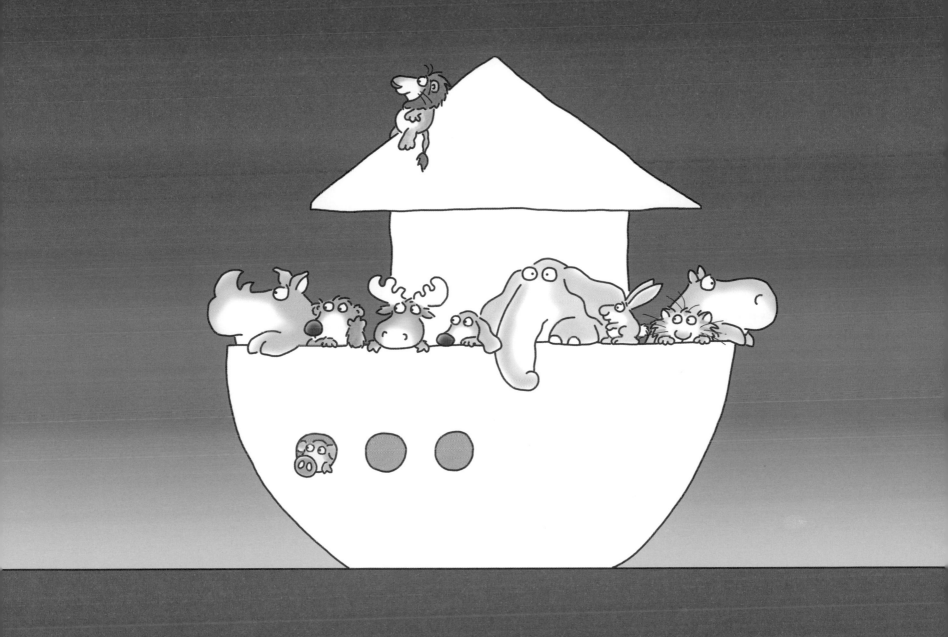

Now everybody

goes below

to take a bath
in one big tub
with soap all over—
SCRUB SCRUB SCRUB!

They hang their towels
on the wall

big

and
small.

With some on top
and some beneath,
they brush and brush
and brush their teeth.

And when the moon is

on the rise, they all go up

to exercise!

And down once more,
but not so fast,
they're on their way
to bed at last.

They
climb
into
their
feather
bed—

some at the foot,

some at the head.

Two little
rabbits
sing a song

The cats and the bears, the li-ons and dogs, the rhi-nos and moose come a-long.

ritard

Two rab-bits (that's we two) will glad-ly a-gree to sing ev-'ry-one's dream in a song.

The day is done.
They say good night,
and somebody
turns off the light.

The moon is high.

The sea is deep.

They rock

and rock

and rock

to sleep.